Text copyright © 1985 Mildred Pitts Walter. Illustrations copyright © 1985 by Diane and Leo Dillon.

Printed in the United States of America.   First Edition

1 2 3 4 5 6 7 8 9 10

Library of Congress Cataloging in Publication Data   Walter, Mildred Pitts.   Brother to the wind.
Summary: With the help of Good Snake, a young African boy gets his dearest wish.   [1. Africa—Fiction.
2. Flying—Fiction.   3. Wishes—Fiction]   I. Dillon, Leo, ill.   II. Dillon, Diane, ill.   III. Title.
PZ7.W17125Br   1985   [E]   83-26800   ISBN 0-688-03811-5   ISBN 0-688-03812-3 (lib. bdg.)
Typography by Kathleen Westray

B·R·O·T·H·E·R
T·O T·H·E W·I·N·D

by Mildred Pitts Walter

pictures by Diane and Leo Dillon

LOTHROP, LEE & SHEPARD BOOKS
New York

TO
HASHIM
IFEYINWA
CHIENYENWA
UCHENNA
M. P. Walter

TO
R. WILLIAM BYNUM
D. & L. Dillon

"GOOD SNAKE can make any wish come true," Emeke's grandmother often said. And every day in the village of Eronni, Emeke herded his
family's goats and dreamed of finding Good Snake. He wanted to make a wish
to fly.

Emeke rose early to herd the goats high up on the mountain. Dark clouds clung to the earth. Morning was almost like night. The rains would soon come.

"Say, Emeke," Ndumu shouted in the dim light, "still want to fly like a bird?" Other boys on the road laughed.

"Our friend thinks he can move like the wind," Mongo said.

"No, he really thinks he will find Good Snake and that Good Snake will help him fly." Nizam's words brought great bursts of laughter.

High up on the mountain, alone with his goats, Emeke looked out at the farms and his village below. Fires blazed and sent up smoke as the men cleared thick brush for new farmland. They worked hard to beat the rains. Their clothes, the colors of the rainbow, flowed with the wind.

Finally Emeke sat watching his goats eat greedily. Then, with his knees drawn to his chest and chin, he closed his eyes. He tried to imagine now what he had often felt in dreams. He wanted to feel the wind, to soar up, up, up, then wheel off like a bird. But his mind filled only with the laughter of his friends.

Then he remembered his grandmother's words: "If you find Good Snake, he will help you fly."

If only I could leave my goats for one day, he thought. I would go searching deep in the bush for Good Snake. But Father would never let me do that.

Maybe he should go into the bush at night when the village was asleep. No boy would go there after dark. Secrets of the bush unfold, and the silence of ghosts grows loud in the dark. No. No boy would do that. "But no boy in my village can fly," Emeke said aloud.

He would find Good Snake and make his wish.

Suddenly he heard a low rumbling noise. What could it be? Not thunder. Thunder came only with the rains. Emeke put his ear closer to the ground and heard the sound of many feet.

Then Emeke saw the strangest thing. A swarm of fireflies moved in a circle in the distance. In their light Emeke saw animals moving toward a tree, not too far from where his goats were feeding.

Emeke jumped up. He saw Elephant, Rhinoceros, Giraffe, and Zebra. He moved closer and saw smaller animals: Turtle, Hyena, Wild Dog, and Hare. There were many birds too. How peacefully and quietly they all moved together. Emeke's goats were calm, still eating the short grass. They will be safe for a little while, Emeke thought.

Curious, he hurried.

Cautiously he fell in line with the animals.

When they reached the tree he saw an unusual thing.

A huge snake was wrapped around the biggest branch. His tail was hidden in the leaves, but his head hung down toward the ground. Emeke's heart beat wildly, his skin went hot, then cold, and his scalp tingled. This is Good Snake, he thought. Emeke wanted to run away, but his feet felt rooted to the spot.

Hyena, Elephant, Rhinoceros, and all the animals, one by one, made wishes. But Turtle stood off to the side, laughing. He did not believe in Good Snake.

As Emeke watched Turtle laughing, he thought of Ndumu, Nizam, and Mongo. Would he dare ask to fly like a bird?

Finally Good Snake nodded at him. Emeke knew it was now his turn. "Oh, Good Snake, I would like to fly."

Good Snake uncurled his tail and brought forth a rock. "Are you sure you want to fly?"

"Oh, yes, Good Snake," Emeke whispered, hardly able to speak.

Good Snake held out the rock. "This is what you must do: Before the rains come, find the bark of a baobab tree and three large bamboo poles. Then make a kite exactly like the one on the back of this rock."

Emeke took the rock and placed it in his pouch. But what did a rock and a kite have to do with flying, Emeke wondered. He wanted to say, Why make a kite? All I want to do is fly like a bird. Instead he listened as Good Snake went on: "Before the feast of the harvest, you must find the right wind for the kite."

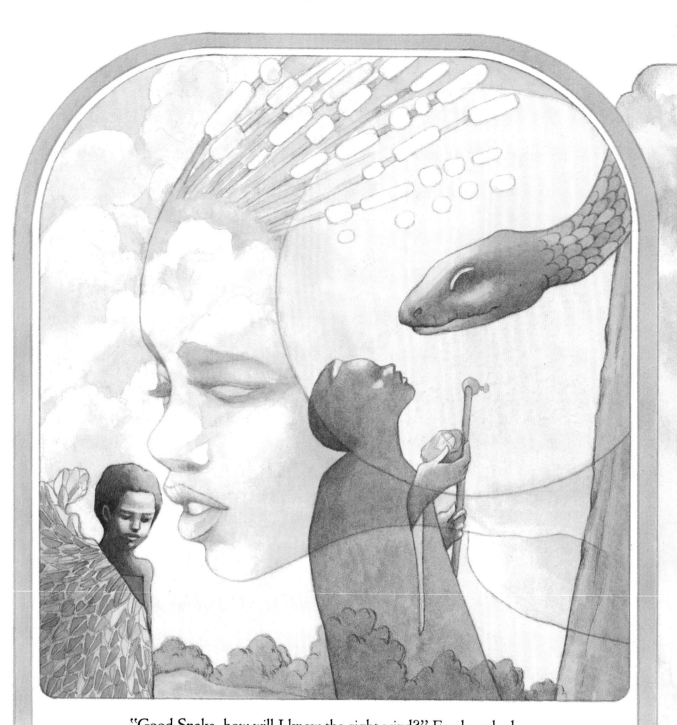

"Good Snake, how will I know the right wind?" Emeke asked.

Good Snake curled up his tail again and looked at Emeke. "The right wind will whisper words that will let you know for sure. Then, on the day of the feast, meet me high on the mountaintop. If you have done all the things that I have asked, then on that day you will fly. One other thing: Keep that rock with you always. It will help you."

Emeke was so happy and excited he almost forgot to thank Good Snake as he hurried back to his goats.

Good Snake called after him. "Be sure you find the bark and bamboo before the rains come."

Turtle laughed. "He, he, he. Beware! Things without wings don't fly."

The dark heavy clouds threatened to overflow. Emeke hurried toward his goats, wondering how he would find bark and bamboo before it rained. He touched the rock and remembered: *The rock will help you.*

When he reached the place where his goats were feeding, he saw Hyena lurking nearby. Emeke hurriedly gathered his goats together to protect them. His goats did not seem at all alarmed. They kept right on eating greedily.

Hyena moved closer.

Emeke became more frightened, and touched the rock.

"Do not be scared," Hyena shouted. "I have come to herd your goats."

"*You?* Herd my goats?" Emeke asked in disbelief.

"Yes. I wished to have more patience and less greed. Be off to the bush to find your bamboo and bark. I'll care for your goats until you return."

Emeke did not trust Hyena.

He was still afraid.

Hyena sensed Emeke's fear and said, "Do you believe Good Snake can help you fly?"

Emeke realized he did not know whether he could trust Good Snake. But his grandmother believed in Good Snake. "Yes," he said. "I believe Good Snake can help me fly."

"Then believe that he can make me a goat herder."

Every few feet Emeke turned to look back, thinking his goats would be eaten. But Hyena was moving among the goats as a caring herder should. I must trust Hyena, he thought, and hurried on toward the bush.

The clouds made the bush almost as dark as night. Emeke stumbled along in the unfriendly quiet.

He must find the bark and bamboo before the rains came.

Suddenly he walked into something that felt like a wall. It moved. Emeke's heart beat wildly. Then he knew. It was not a wall at all. It was Elephant. Emeke was frightened; he squeezed the rock for comfort.

"I am here to help you find the baobab tree," Elephant said.

"How do you know I need bark from the baobab tree?"

"I made a wish too. I wished to be kind and helpful. My wish can come true, if I can help you." Elephant led the way into the bush.

Soon Emeke had enough bark for his kite. Emeke thanked Elephant. Now he must hurry to find the bamboo. His father would be furious if he found the goats left in Hyena's care.

At last Emeke found the watering hole where bamboo grew. To his surprise, Rhinoceros was waiting for him with three neatly cut poles.

"I knew you would come," Rhinoceros said. "I made a wish to be gentle and of service. My wish has come true."

It was night when Emeke returned to the pasture. His goats were gone! Emeke's heart skipped beats. He felt weak and his head seemed to swell. He ran here and there, everywhere, looking. Then, around a curve, he saw his goats. Hyena had gathered them all together.

The goats pushed and shoved around Emeke. Hyena was glad to see Emeke too. Emeke thanked Hyena and hurried down the mountain.

He had not gone far when he saw his father with men from the village. Emeke's friends were with them.

"Where were you?" his father demanded.

"On the mountain."

"No, you were not!" Ndumu shouted.

"We looked all over for you," Nizam said.

"And what is this burden you are carrying?" His father pointed to the bark and bamboo.

"I want to fly, Father, so— "

An explosion of laughter interrupted Emeke. Emeke looked at his father and knew his father was humiliated. The men laughed because they thought Emeke was a lazy, careless boy who did not take his duties seriously.

"Why do you say foolish things, Emeke?" his father demanded. "Did you ever see humans fly?"

Emeke felt his father was more hurt than angry. He wanted to move closer to his father, but it was as though the laughter had turned him to stone.

Finally, with tears in his voice and with great respect, Emeke tried to explain again.

"Father, I did not leave the goats alone. Hyena cared for them...."

There was another explosion of laughter. Over the laughter Emeke's father shouted, "Let me hear no more of this foolishness. Now, I want you to promise that you will never leave the goats unattended again."

Emeke remembered that he still had to find the right wind. He did not want to promise.

"Emeke," his father said, "if you leave the goats again, I will have to punish you. I want your word that you will not."

"I promise," Emeke said sadly.

Later that night, thunder rumbled and lightning lit up the village. Emeke heard the sound of drops like small pebbles pelting the roof. The rains had come. He had found the bark and bamboo just in time.

Rain fell in gray sheets, soaking the earth, filling the streams. Emeke could not herd his goats. While other children sat around the fire roasting maize and groundnuts, Emeke sat alone working on his kite.

With the rock close by, he worked every day. Soon word spread about the huge kite. Emeke's friends called him bird boy, wing-flapper. People in the village said Emeke was a foolish boy. His family was ashamed of him. Only his grandmother believed he might fly one day.

"Why such a heavy kite?" his mother asked.

"You will never fly that one on a string," his father said.

"It will fly me. I will soar in the wind, dive and wheel like a bird without falling," Emeke said proudly.

His grandmother beamed, but his father said, "Put the kite away. Forget this flying foolishness."

Finally the rain fell in drops as thin as needles against the sunlight. White clouds raced away, leaving the sky clean and blue. The sun shone bright and the wind blew cold. Emeke herded his goats at the foot of the mountain and wondered where he would ever find the right wind.

Days grew warmer. After many days and nights, the growing season ended and it was time for the harvest to begin.

The night before the harvest festival, the moon rose like a giant orange
ball. The night slowly turned almost as bright as day.

Emeke lay listening to the wind. "Come out, come out, you don't have
to break your promise," the wind sighed.

Emeke rushed outside. He hurried to the edge of his village. The grass
grew tall, and the wind sang like the sound of the sea. The grass bowed left and
right, moving like women's skirts in the dance. Emeke stood still, listening.

Then softly as the flutter of a bird's wing came a whisper: "My brother."
Emeke trembled with the excitement that comes with dancing. Be still and listen,
he told himself. Again the whisper: "My brother." That is the right wind! He
felt light with happiness.

The rest of the night, Emeke slept without dreaming.

The morning of the festival came with the sound of many drums. The air
was heavy with excitement. Today I will fly, Emeke thought when he awoke.

Emeke walked with his family to the center of the village. His friends gathered around him, excited about the games and races to be held at the festival.

"I will fly today," Emeke said matter-of-factly. "Look up and you will see me."

"Then look down," Ndumu said. "Oooh, no more Emeke! He is splattered like a bird's egg." Ndumu fell to the ground, arms and legs spread. All the boys bent with laughter.

"I will fly. You will see," Emeke said.

When the center of the village was overrun with people, Emeke slipped away with his kite and rock. He hurried up the mountain to meet Good Snake.

As he came near the top of the mountain, he heard a plodding sound. He looked around and saw Turtle struggling to join him.

"Hey," Turtle shouted. "Beware! Boys were not made to fly."

"With the help of Good Snake, I can, and I will."

"What if you drift to the end of the earth or land on your feet in the mouth of Crocodile, or in Lion's lair?"

Emeke became frightened. He had thought only of flying. Then suddenly he heard the wind sighing softly. Emeke's confidence returned. "I am not afraid, Turtle." He hurried to find Good Snake.

High up on the mountain Good Snake was waiting.

"I made the kite and found the wind," Emeke said to Good Snake.

Good Snake turned the kite this way and that to make sure it was made well, safe for flying. Then he led Emeke to the edge of the mountain. "You will fly from here down into your village."

Emeke heard the drums from the distance. He looked down and saw the cloud of dust from dancing feet. He thought of Ndumu's words and of his friends' laughter. Turtle's words echoed: "Boys are not made to fly." Emeke hurriedly backed away from the edge. He looked at Good Snake and said, "I cannot fly."

"But everything is ready."

"With all those people in the center of the village, where will I land safely?" Emeke cried.

"You must think of nothing but flying. Trust me with the rest. Give me the rock. I leave you with the wind."

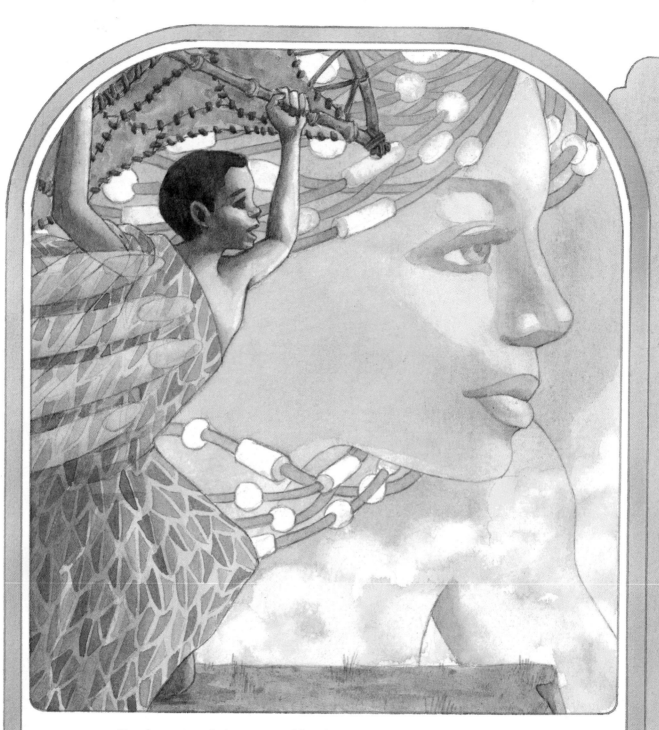

Emeke pointed the nose of his kite up slightly. Should he trust Good Snake? Would he really fly? He waited. He listened.

"My brother," the wind sighed.

Emeke felt the easy, steady wind. He forgot his fear. He balanced his kite and started running toward the edge of the mountain.

He kept his mind on running and keeping his kite's nose up.

Suddenly he was in the air. He flowed up, then floated down, gliding with the wind. His body seemed to disappear. There was only wind, sky, and the earth far below. He was flying! Soaring, turning, streaming down, then lightly, easily floating. "I am brother to the wind," he shouted.

He floated to his feet as lightly as a feather. His grandmother was the first to reach him. She hugged him, beaming with love. His mother and father smiled with pride. All of his friends rushed to examine the kite. "He did fly like a bird," Nizam said.

Drummers beat their drums, sending up sounds as great as all the thunder in the world. Dancing feet sent up clouds of dust. Emeke danced to the rhythms with his grandmother.

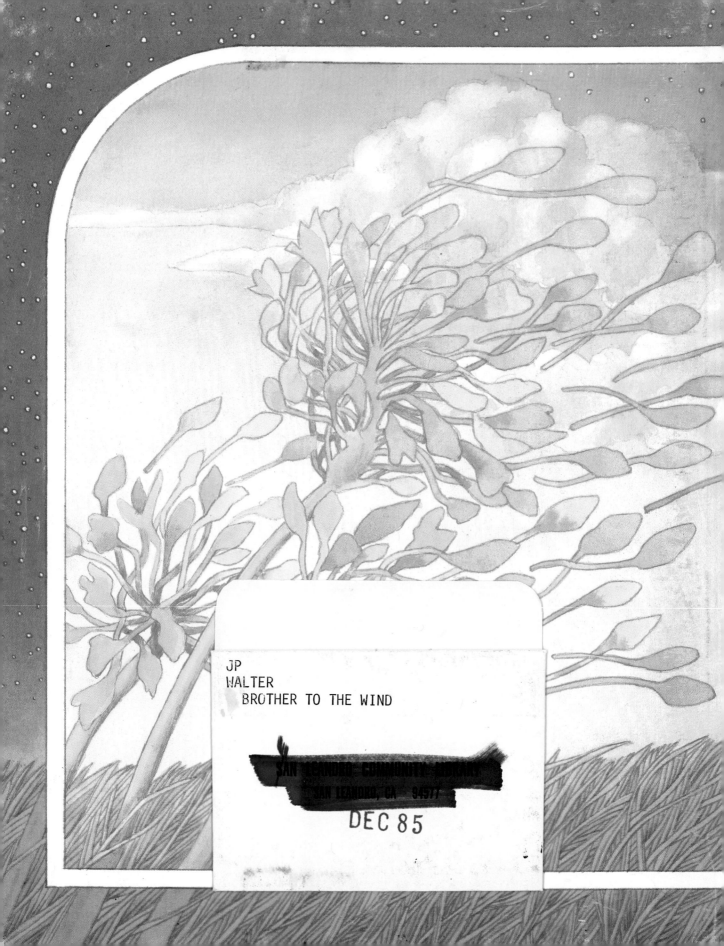